THE SIX LEGGED SPIDER OF MEMORY AND SOME OTHER DRIVEL

Rocky van de Benderskum

by String and I

CONTENTS

Title Page

Copyright

The 'F' WORD

Preface

The Six Legged Spider of Memory '   1

Dyhydrogen Monoxide   5

Nunya   8

WARNING-WARNIng WARNING   9

The tunnel   12

The red death?   13

Deliberate misinformation   15

The great 2020 bogroll fiasco   16

The ghosts of Saturday night as observed by a random   18
horned sheep eating marijuana trim, at 'NaPoLeo

Marijuana   21

String keeps me sane   23

Work   24

Purple   26

In a world of need we don't need greed   27

Activist poetrickist   30

A Resourced Based Economy   31

What don't you understand? 33

THE EXTINCTION CRISIS 34

Benderskum Thoughts 37

Bollotics 40

No more plant based 42

Numbers 44

Not Vegan Because 47

Nonsensical 49

Land of Hopeless Tory 51

How did we all get here, how has this become? 53

Harvest festival Crops not Shops 55

Gobbledegook; 56

The World needs a hand 58

Even more drivel 63

Be seventeenth hemp tester 66

Food for the future 69

Eat the Government 71

Crops not shops 74

Bollocks To Drums 76

#Artynot 78

Just because I can 80

Afterword 85

About The Author 87

Books By This Author 89

THE 'F' WORD

Well here it is yet another pile of utter tosh for you to damge your brains with or not if you follow the rule of;

Not reading it but goin upstairs on a double decker bus and throwing it at a passing lorry which will with any luck render it utterly safe due to the unreadable nature it will have then undertaken.

If you decide not to do this remember to have a biro on you when you do attempt the dangerous action of reading it, the reason for the blank spaces spread around the thing doodle, scribble or whatever you call it in these spaces just to check that you still have some cognitive thigamyjigs to hand

And don't forget you matter until you are multiplied by the speed of light squared then you energy

PREFACE

What does that even mean preface is it the layers of soft tissue underneath the face or is it when the room makes a space ready for your face just before you enter.
Lifes so full of mysteries

THE SIX LEGGED
SPIDER OF MEMORY

One evening well actually kind of early hours after some late night revelling in the local park Florence the spider arrived home at the spider house opened the spider door with the spider key went in and sat down in the spider chair by the spider fire, completely exhausted. So he thought he'd just read a bit of the spider book before bed, then he realised two of his legs were missing. Ok at this point I think it's fair to say that one or two of you may have got the impression that the spider was female I'd further like to point out that the thought is very namist of you, I'm sure that was the word.

Anyway back to Florence he decided to go back to the park and search for them, he looked in all the places he'd been even managed to grab a couple of his mates to help him look but to no avail. The next day he went to the library and built a little spider tent you know those things we all call webs, not those they are tents, no proper big grand spider colonies where all eight legged creatures are welcomed now they are webs that's where all the knowledge of everything ever past, present and future is stored we humans if we've even herd of it call it the Akashic Hall of Records. But that's way into the future

While he was there he was researching genetics so he could clone new legs he thought but ended up just reading everything. There's always plenty of food for a spider in a library humans leave bits of food everywhere, it's quite disgusting unless you're a spider or a detritivore then its normal.

So he read and read everything and remembered it all.

I know right?

My head would ex...plode.

Spiders have really complicated brain patterns and can instantly sum at once about 100 different subjects, and actually concentrate on all of them which would explain the sometimes wonky way they walk and because of their inter-dimensional jiggery pokery.

He became so engrossed in knowledge and philosophy and the arts, he forgot his missing legs and even his name; he became known as the 6 legged spider of memory and was happy with the name. Once he knew and understood everything his passion became to impart that essence of knowing to everybody.

So being a spider and as such maybe not that well explained previously only partially in this dimension, hence the movement.

He became the first ever six legged spider of memory this is centuries ago when the world was still waking up and people hadn't done their best to destroy it so he tried first to get a leaders attention with the aim of imparting that knowledge. He was not only partially in another dimension but also really tiny. He crawled up the side of the bed of the sleeping leaders left ear. I'm not sure why but always left though. That other dimensiony bit first then by a process of inter dimensional jiggery pokery swapping aboutabishness, he was soon chatting to the subconscious mind of the first ever knowing for pineal particle and humanity segment transfer subject. He came up with a way to impart the knowledge of everything to that mind unfortunately it turned out to be faulty and the usb S that the spider had developed in his tent at the library was snapped off in mid everything so the first leader could only ever know half of anything and therefore philosophically so could future leaders, which actually explains quite a lot.

So the spider went back to the library which had by now been closed until further notice, like many other libraries across the country, because they didn't make enough dosh for the posh. While he'd been gone another spider had come across the place a female called Colin named after her grandmother, she also only had six legs. The six legged spider of memory (six for short) asked her what happened, she told him losing the two legs saved her life as she fell in a fire and pushed herself up with two legs. Wow said six that's such a story, you are lucky to be here. Anyway blah, blah, blah boy girl blah, blah, blah, then they had lots of little spiders there so they all set about learning everthink, everydun, everywas and everywillbe.

Some went off to start new webs in disused libraries and factories which were becoming more and more common.

Nowadays the new breed of six legged spiders of memory use a much more technical approach to knowledge impartation and stuff extraction they teleport, both directions through about seven different dimensions to make it instantaneous, virtually painless and almost completely safe. Going in via the ear was always a little bit yucky even for spiders. This has now gone on for millennia and the spider civilisations worldwide are all connected magnetically.

Now comes the part which most parents may need to cover their ears for as they are probably too squeamish.

In fact kids tell your parents to go and drink some sherry or make a cup of tea or plant some Dahlias or some other grown up nonsense.

The very first human to spider interaction back in the day set a universal genetic precedent or law of nature if you prefer that would be carried on due to the multi dimensional nature of such things, blah, blah, blah.

We would host them for a short period of our lives, right at the beginning before even cognizant, cognussant, cognosence, ah proper thought patterns arose. That short period between; new born and actual person, the Glop stage I call it. However a bargain was struck on that day that has sewn repercussions throughout our time on this planet, the bargain was the knowing of everything for a shred of your reality and a piece of your pineal gland or third eye.

Some people have always been impervious and have kept their pineal glands intact stayed real and learned everything they know over time or sometimes by a chance encounter.

Anyway nowadays things are much different the whole operation is done by teleportation and elec-tic-tok which is actually a marvellous way to travel one which I would urge you to try if you ever get the opportunity.

Even though only it's only the really small spiders that can do the mind knowledge malarkey the teleportation is just a thing and everyone can learn, but it takes a lot of training, but like I said oh so worth it.

For instance even the very first thing you have to learn is gruelling;

Hear the colour orange while smelling the colour blue and feeling the colour green but seeing purple but not as a colour as an entity in itself. Like I said the very first thing but...

Blah, blah, blah, boring

You get four hours to complete the first task and it only gets harder the second task is learn the phrase;

'Don't Pass Audit Prg, Uber Liebe René's Caine, Master, Master'

You have one hour, which leads to the third task you have eternity to explain the meaning of the previous phrase. Once you've done that the teleportation process is a cinch, spiders can instinctively just do it, which is how sometimes you get one appear out of nowhere in the middle of the room right before your eyes.

Good luck with your training if you intend to try your luck

DYHYDROGEN MONOXIDE

Why do people feel that the moon affects them?

I'll tell you but need to pint because it rhymes I use the word phlegm

Phew that's better, disgusting I know but I have bad lung capacity

Luckily I'm usually so charming and it doesn't affect my vivacity

Now what was I saying oh yeah the moon

Has been known to turn people into a loon

The moon is in orbit because of magnets and that isn't just pi in the sky

No it's not even about trigonometry its magnetism, no word of a lie

The earth apparently is in orbit too although we're going round the sun

Sounds to me like round the bend but that's just my brain having fun

I'm not a clever geezer so it may not be proper truze

Unlike the stuff in The Red Book of Nollidge but outside we all get to choose

I seem to have gone off at a tangent to be honest that's often the case

The more baffling this world just gets daily is why I'm losing the human race

Oh yeah back to the human and the rule of the moon

Yes back to the science which didn't happen too soon

People are made of sixty per cent water and forty of other stuff

Go and sit in a dehumidifier if you want to call my bluff

Though it isn't a bluff it's fact

And then again I'm off my track

Two parts hydrogen is a part of water

Add one of Oxygen whether tall or shorter

Hydrogen is positive and because of that attracts
Oxygen which is negative by magnetic that's a fact
Like poles repel but these are not alike
All that water sloshing about while riding on my bike
Tides as well it seems are in this magnetic field
Water, water everywhere I hope the truth revealed
Plants too are affected in this magnetised water mix
Magnetism once again playing its magnetrix
During photosynthesis a vacuum is created
So the magnetised water rises up to fill the space vacated
The moon it seems and its phases make me a little crazy
It's very complicated scientific stuff and my physics is a little hazy
Maybe I was already mad and the moon was just an excuse
When water enters an animal the name for it is perfuse
Water enters by osmosis at least if it enters a plant
 I'd like to explain that fully to you but I'm sorry I simply can't
I'd like to explain it fully but then I would have to kill you
Instead I'll leave you to look it up the research will undoubtedly thrill you
I may not have explained it all but I had a little fun
Cos I ain't a clever science bod I'm just a benderskum

NUNYA

Who am I? Why should you care? I'm as mischievous as my lack of hair
I'll do you no harm and I'm not short of charm
But beware of my cynical tongue
I'm actual an optimist or something that rhymes like this
It is what it is, I might take the piss
But I'm not the only one
And maybe I do it for fun
So now who are you? Where do you live? What do you do?
You can trust me it's true, I wouldn't harm you
Is it rude to ask? What is your pin code?
Pass me those bullets I'm empty and needing a reload
What that's all about I've no fucking idea
My mouth says the words that the computer types here
So don't blame me for writing this drivel, no, it isn't me you should blame
No it's String my invisible friend, I think the fuckers insane

WARNING-WARNING
WARNING

Please be aware for your own peace of mind, that there is a clownin this book so just close your eyes and scroll past, or simply don't go there. I for one certainly wouldn't wish to give you the heeby jeebies.

Alternatively however you could also ignore this friendly gesture from your old pal Azazel.

Oops I wasn't intending to reveal that now, if ever, but the proverbial wilderness demon is out of the bag now so to speak.

So I guess it's time to introduce meself;

As I said Azazel's the name, I'm the demon that used to get the goat at Yom Kippur, Which incidentally is one of the few things I dislike about this benderskum, it doesn't eat corpses, what kind of a monster is that, I mean that to me is proper scary stuff, how does it even survive, anyway that's him not me give me the goats back and stop having for dinner they're my scran not yours.

I taught you lot how to make weapons so you could kill each other and cosmetics to make jealousy a thing to use those weapons for and well you all know how impossible it is to stop that ship has long since sailed

Some of you lot call it sinful but trust bruv, its just business and it's all about the dosh, luxurious lifestyles bish, bash, bosh. Anyways never mind all that twaddle we are warning you about the clown thing so you don't go there can't say fairer than that, just so you know Being a demon is probably nothing like you lot think. What in a great big cave with fires all around shrieks, howls, moulten lava pools, explosions, and the demon well me for instance luxuriating in a lava flow spurting out the side of a black cave wall. Yeah well you know health spas and all you lot do them

9

too. Mostly not though that's terrific fun you know playing catch with souls, or kick a feeling oh,I love it yet it does also get tiresome so inhabiting a part of one of you lot is what a lot of us, you aren't aware of it because we don't interfere its against our way and well we just don't.

demoning; its all just about death, destruction, famines, plagues, droughts the fun stuff, but that's just work this inhabiting a humanoid is such fun it's not like I control it. No perish the thought it has complete autonomy, where is the fun in control. We demons do that anyway no this is holiday, I've been inside this err, err, benderskum really for there isn't any other proper definition, it is what it is. of which is a benderskum and my latest symbiosis and of course I must say I likes it, there's a nice feel to it almost human even and intensely caring of its loved ones. I suggest you take some deep breathes and consider this thought benderskum is nice, who loves deeply, he protects what is right fiercely and is a bit of a twat plus he's got an invisible friend called String which is of course fine String's a proper nice geezer drinks Guinness just like a half or he gets too soggy, I met him in Knightsbridge giving churchills to homeless people then apologising to them for it and so he should tight fucking twat he should've given them tenners.

Now it gets worse String it seems has an imaginary friend called Bail. You may feel that's fair enough String is always getting benderskum out of scrapes,

but you know? Or maybe you don't know.

Well this may be betraying a trust but hey I'm a fucking I do this thing called whatever the fuck I want,

so here goes;

String's imaginary friend Bail isn't real, however from the other side benderskum or rocky as some people call it well most actually, is real at least in this dimension its really difficult to explain in such simple terms that exist here. So that still begs the question the writer of this drivel possibly, am I real or not? Is this real or just more fantasy? When I actually read some of the rubbish I write, I'm glad I'm not real.

Now what was I saying...oh yes don't look at his page if you have or suffer from coulrophobia the fear of clowns, actually it's probably too late if you are still reading this, in which case first of all apologies for all that previous twaddle he's just a benderskum and can't help it and bears you no malice of course

But here goes:

Roses are rotting violets are dead

Twisty the clown is there under your bed

I'm off now just to observe from within so to speak in a way understandable it's a bit more, well just more really

I'll hand the reins back to him

Toodle Pip xx

THE TUNNEL

The tunnel was built a Heath Robinson construction
With a wing and a prayer to avoid it's destruction
At first water collapsed flooded the bomb hole
But the crew built a retainer react on a roll
We've had more than our fair share of windy weather
So we tied down our plastic but it broke its tether
The repair had worked but then something new
The wind got right big and tore it in two
So we talked and we chatted and plotted and schemed
A crew came along and worked better than I'd dreamed
Trenches all dug and sand bags in place
Losing the light it became a bit of a race
Now the tunnel is back up again what a relief
After the wind tore through it which beggars belief
And now to my bed I go aching and in pain
But the dream is alive still so I'm again
I was happy with life so this was merely a trial
For this little benderskum that can't help but smile

THE RED DEATH?

When the red death follows and settles on your head
The shops are mostly shut so homo-consumerus doesn't feel fed
Remember then the world we had a world we left for the burning
We took and took and took some more and it's way too late for returning
Or maybe not and what starts with a plot soon blossoms into a garden
That is when your back stops aching and your hands start to harden
Or at least according to Kipling and not the maker of cakes
And I know the name brings that to mind it's a very common mistake
So before we forget it's important to remember the world we had before
Endless opportunities that's is if you knew the score
Worldly wise and practical with where there's a will there's a way
Although with the homogenised version of us, would we make it? It's hard to say
Open the Doors what do you hear nobody gets out of here alive
Maybe not for the first time I realise but that is the way with pop jive
Do you dig or do you not depends on the state of the land
Bony, stony hard dried up clay certainly needs a hand
Feed it, straw and compost and such
If it needs a hand that stuffs like a crutch
Take away but put stuff back it's easy to understand why
When you've used up all the ingredients there's nothing left for the pie
And spraying poisons for pests and diseases just further poisons the land

The top soil dies, so needs chemicals to grow in. Which part don't you understand?
How quickly society seems to have forgotten
The system was failing, corrupt and rotten
Santayana said 'Those who cannot remember the past are condemned to repeat it'.
History is subjective that's why many just try to delete it
So remember the world we had before and don't let go of that thought
Get back to the land and grow your food don't let it come to naught

DELIBERATE MISINFORMATION

To wear a mask or not is more than left to chance
The reason is the government just want us all to dance
And argue with each other therefore ignoring what they're doing
Giving contracts out to mates while the country they are screw-
ing
They'll simply say you must do this unless you are exempt
Or backtrack and say or maybe that obscuring their intent
Whatever they tell you shut your eyes and quickly count to ten
Then if you still believe them do that all over again
Then I hear this vaccination doesn't even have a licence
At first I thought I misheard that but heard the same twice since
The reason the NHS don't prescribe cannabis is because of that
lack
So don't ever believe it's for public health or the government have
got your back
The government are meant to govern not make each other richer
While creating a country of tell tale tits and other curtain
twitchers

THE GREAT 2020 BOGROLL FIASCO

The first great toilet roll depression of 2020
The shelves were all empty although there was plenty
It originated in Australia where the stocks were short
But an overblown social media worldwide news report
Blew the whole damn thing out of proportion
A very cleverly orchestrated media distortion
In Australia most of the loo roll is made in China
So the world shortage was invented by a social panic designer
Making the new world order all about me
Divide and conquer as always can't you see
We had already had too much freedom
The government's started to realise we didn't really need 'em
They were witnessing worldwide an air of dissent
Putting fear into those behind the government
A new world order was dawning the people all went mental
So those in charge came down hard and made us all fragmental
To maintain their status quo needed a very drastic change
The majority stayed home in fear and didn't think it strange
When you panic buy you are following a predetermined pattern
A bit like running a relay race without the usual baton
Eventually in line we stand and do not try to find
A way to make a better world the blind just leading the blind
It's how they rule you see, it's all about mind control
This time started by the fear of having no toilet roll

THE GHOSTS OF SATURDAY NIGHT AS OBSERVED BY A RANDOM HORNED SHEEP EATING MARIJUANA TRIM, AT 'NAPOLEONE'S AFTER HOURS PIZZA HOUSE'

One day a very chilled random sheep was eating marijuana trim
Some people came along angrily and said these things to him
Marijuana is a racist word we don't really think you should eat it
It's just a pile of trim he said I think you lot should beat it
At that he continued to eat his trim ignoring the diddley eye dinlows
And gazed at the morning sunlight appearing through the pizza house windows
He looks around with wonder and a joyful child's delight
To see the dawning of the day and the breaking of the night
Oi! Charlie what're you doing? You're not trying to roll a spliff
Hey Norma remind him it's really late so his fingers must be stiff
Is that a Nickerbocker Glory or just a bloody sundae?
I know the News is a pack of Lies but I'm pretty sure its Monday
And you Goodfella what're you up to trying to Blow me down?
Stuffing your face with toast in your jammies and dressing gown
The pit and the pendulum comes to mind and a streetcar named

desire

And a gay guy who painted a tin of soup and Zombieland has it's town crier

But eating eyeballs with chopsticks is more than a little bit rough

Resistance is futile that's blatant from that pizza you continue to stuff

And you my pretty my lovely you're what it's all about

There's something I first have to tell you then you'll know of it, that I've no doubt

Forever joyful when you can take

Those special mushrooms home to bake

The following lines have been removed because of some sensitive issue

Something about Mohamed Abdullahi Mohamed and a place called Mogadishu

Ah here we are back to our regular uncensored service

I can't remember where we were or if there was a purpose

The sheep continues to munch marijuana and hopes that it was worth it

First black, then green, then yellow right next to forty two

Red, yellow taxi, purple and in the garage blue

Then the washer up guy like a sawn off waitress comes out waving an axe

Whilst the old guy across the street is buying a brand new set of facts

Then you realise you've really had enough

It's time to invent a big box of stuff

Inside it you need to keep the part of you that's real

Which the inevitable creeping memory moth is very keen to steal

So keep it safe but don't hide it for wherever you may go

Is where you are eventually its inevitable don't you know

So if you pucker up and then knuckle down

Meet your own ghosts with a smile not a frown

You'll know it was all a thing of the past and maybe best forgotten

There was never a king of punk and certainly not Johnnie Rotten

Anyway I think I'll just sign off from here I don't wish to blah,
blah, blah, blah
I realise that this poem could be the problem so I'll end it and just
say Tata

MARIJUANA

When they heard of a plant that grew like a weed
 With the most nutritious edible seed
Its medicinal properties were second to none
Tens of thousands of uses and then, still some
Can be made into bricks that are carbon sinks
Which could clean up the air but they still didn't think
Could be spun into fabric for clothes and more
Well at least that's how it was before
No, they made it illegal to own or consume
And don't plant that seed it's illegal to bloom
So now they just follow an ancient lie
It's a dangerous drug so they'll pass it on by
Medicinal value it has none,
So that's why they put it in schedule one.
A bunch of lies, not an inkling of truth
That they hold onto now despite all the proof
Except when they're wearing the other suit
Or whichever one brings them more of the loot
They grow it themselves with complete autonomy
Whilst denying it to us...how can that ever be?
They care about profit and they're lying to you
You know deep down that's what they always do
They ignore the truth while changing the rules
Continuing to believe we're a bunch of fools
Whoever made up this licence to grow?
With an underhand handshake if you're in the know
The swish of an apron strikes a hammer on chisel
I'll cut to the chase it's a bit of a swizzle
Historically they told everyone Cannabis was bad
That bubble has burst that fact makes me glad

The world is much wiser than it was way back when
And soon we'll have Cannabis growing again,
Out in the open where it ought to be
Not hidden in closets, but proud and free
Fields of hemp repairing the earth
Showing we care knowing its worth
Starting to repair all the things we have broken
Much bigger than us not just merely a token
Don't think of replacing, a whole innovation
A thoughtful caring human nation
Replenish, Renew, Rethink, Refresh and maybe even Repair
If we did stuff very differently we might just have a prayer
I could go on about this till kingdom fucking comes
But who the fuck listens to a benderskum

STRING KEEPS ME SANE

I'm lucky String is always on hand to set me right
Giving me homeostasis in mind, body and psyche
Three of us together and not even a crowd
We have a silent friend but he's not very loud
If you do on occasion get lonely I suggest invent a friend
Don't invent too many though or they'll drive you round the bend
I know this from experience in a time called way back when
They drove me round the bend alright but drove me back again

WORK

Sitting in the polytunnel watching all the work
Difficult enough as I is not a one to shirk
But breathing isn't easy and my heart goes fast as fuck
So I try my best to sit and rest and not just push my luck
But you lot were amazing sorting out the ground
Moving all the compost and spreading it around
Planting all the seedlings filling the place with life
Growing food for the future will get us through the strife
Even if you are comfortably off and think this isn't you
Life would be so much more bearable if I were the same as you
But diversity is everything and shouldn't be a choice
The perplexities could be endless when everything has a voice
Never mind our differences I am the same as you
Another human being in this state enlisted zoo
Babylon the mighty Babylon the great
Babylon the master that puts food on our plate
So is food an addiction as well as an actual necessity?
Socially engineered perhaps to create the present Globesity
Whoever controls the food controls it all or so I've been told
But that was something never right even in the good old bad days
of old
Food for free if its up to me the way it fucking ought to be
You see? There ain't anything wrong with anarchy

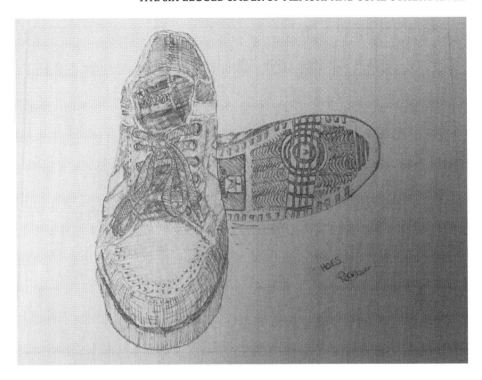

PURPLE

I do indeed wear purple some say a tad too much
I believe that's a matter of taste each to their own or such
I could also have worn orange but then I'd just look Dutch
Or perhaps a suit of silver but maybe that's too much
Either way I love my purple and nothing rhymes with it
Not even in my poems which I know are a little shit
Whenever I have people round did you guess I'm a cannibal
Whenever people visited I ate them one and all
As for reading papers I'm behind on current affairs
I don't like to read all that doom and gloom and realise that no one really cares
I've heard people say I march to the sound of a different drumbeat
However for a start I'm telling it straight these just ain't marching feet
So if you can't stand my offbeat ways I suggest you just move along
To make matters worse for that drumbeat I don't even have a drum
I'm just a guy that writes poems and also wears a hat
A proper Italian fedora and what's more; purple at that

IN A WORLD OF NEED WE DON'T NEED GREED

Everything in moderation
It gives us everything we need,
Somewhere to live and thrive and succeed
It gives us plants it gives us trees,
 Fertile lands and wondrous seas
But the human virus is the worst disease
And we've brought this planet to its knees
We've stripped away lots and put back a bit
As for biodiversity we don't give a shit
They tell us we've only got 12 years NO more
To sort it all out and even the score
But in my opinion it's too little too late
Those horses have bolted through the open gate
Just like a virus moving into a cell
We are making our planet a living hell
When we've used up everything that we can see
I expect we'll be hoping for 'Planet B'
When I look at my world I just shed a tear
Cos most of you fuckers don't want to hear
You recycle plastic and paper and tins
And what can't be reused goes in landfill bins
But is that enough as our world starts to die
No just drive your car and continue to fly
I'm doing my bit I cannot do more
Blah, blah, blah I've heard it before
The world can repair itself of that there's no doubt
But we won't be here to sing, talk or shout
We'll be long gone extinct just like the dinosaur

Without the effects of a giant meteor
It won't be too long till we're buried in plastic
PLEASE listen to this these words aren't bombastic
We are using our planet as a means to an end
But when something is broken it's important to mend
There are holes in the sky where radiation gets in
And when it does it will burn your skin
Because these holes are fat while our atmospheres thin
The holes were all made by human pollution
So to clean up our act is the sensible solution
We can't keep on taking without putting back
When it's empty it's empty and that is a fact
Were cutting down trees, polluting air, sea and soil
And surprise, surprise we're addicted to oil
That particular oil comes from way underground
But there's other oil that is easily found
For there is a plant with wondrous seeds
That can help us and all of our planetary needs
We have never needed fossil oils
They pollute our atmosphere and seas and soils
There is a plant with amazing yields
That we could be planting in our fields
Our planet is fragile we don't need to break her
There's oil from this plant 300 gallons an acre
As if that's not enough to make oil companies sour
After extraction there's 6 tons of flour
And medicine, building blocks and all sorts of things,
Eco safe plastic and paper and string
The list is quite endless as you'll quickly see
But what is that plant what could it be?
The plants name is cannabis but don't be alarmed
It's been here forever and it's not here to harm
It's been here forever it followed us round
It could clean up the air and puts food in the ground
So why don't we use this to help with our needs
The answer is simply put corporate greed

They made it illegal to own or consume
But I don't believe them and won't dance to their tune
They tell us its bad and say it's a pest
While hidden in plain view feather their nests
So heed what is said and grow all those seeds
Or just sit and watch telly as our home planet bleeds
So pretend that I'm lying when I say all this stuff
Cos to hear and ignore is really too tough
Our world is in peril there may be no next bit
No 'Planet B' and certainly no exit
Bill Hicks once called us a virus with shoes
So you just keep consuming and I'll just sing the blues

ACTIVIST POETRICKIST

Cannabis, poetry, news and activism seems a strange combination
Although they fit really well during our present herbal castration
Obsolete laws, not fit for purpose, quite in need of cessation
Then we can make smoking a spliff more than mere assignation
Wake up politicians make some proper laws then you'll cause celebration
Cannabis, poetry, news and activism seems a perfect combination
With a New weed order blooming in sight across this human nation
They are fully on the run and don't know where to turn
Watch and wait we're winning as they have begun to learn
Court room trials are crumbling without that burden of proof
That cannabis is schedule one hasn't a grain of truth
So hear us UK government I care not if it's abrupt
Everyone knows it's a political scam cos you lot are corrupt

A RESOURCED BASED ECONOMY

A band of Eco Warriors decided to grow some food
So they dug up the gardens of strangers which actually sounds quite rude
But that was not their intention so chill and listen relax
Until you're in possession of all the relevant facts
The food they were growing or planting was for the greater good
Recycling bottles and building things with stuff like palette wood
They'll also if you ask them give you growing advice
And though some of them look quite scary they're really very nice
During the lockdowns many stayed at home but some are now getting out
So now more than ever they need more help so this why I shout
They are a growing community and would love to welcome you too
If you cannot support them physically there is lots more you can do
People often ask advice and they are happy to help if they know
Maybe a place in which you could help but there's plenty more seeds to sow
They are nowadays renting a greenhouse but for that there is rent to be paid
So they set up a whatchamacallit? a more fiscal way to give aid
They are a growing community but cannot do this alone
I know this is asking for money I can already hear people moan
But they are a growing community and you could be part of it too
So have a think then maybe follow the link the rest is up to you

One Love

https://www.facebook.com/groups/824963631333587

WHAT DON'T YOU UNDERSTAND?

Stop, get the fuck out of your car,
take off your shoes and walk on the land
The hard times are coming it's hard to deny
Look at the climate look at the sky
Eventually they'll cut down most of the trees
And the ones that are left will be full of disease
Thousand of species will go extinct every year
But the average citizen still won't care
There'll be Flora museums and Fauna zoos
When the natural has gone and nothings renewed
With their GM seeds they'll try to grow food
But with GM seeds plantings too crude
Those seeds need the chemicals made out of oil
They were never designed to grow just in soil
There'll soon be no oil even for cars
Unless they discover a supply on Mars
With the air too polluted and food really short
They'll look to the pasts ignored lessons taught
By then it's too late and there's no turning back
Too late to fix it or pick up the slack

There will still be roads from this place to that
But no life in sight not even a cat

THE EXTINCTION CRISIS

We are losing so many species at such an incredible rate that scientists are calling this the sixth mass extinction. We're currently experiencing the worst spate of species die-offs since the loss of the dinosaurs 65 million years ago. Although extinction is a natural phenomenon, it occurs at a natural "background" rate of about one to five species per year.

Scientists estimate we're now losing species at 1,000 to 10,000 times the background rate, with literally dozens going extinct every day. It could be a scary future indeed, with as many as 30 to 50 percent of all species possibly heading toward extinction by mid-century.

Unlike past mass extinctions, caused by events like asteroid strikes, volcanic eruptions, and natural climate shifts, the current crisis is almost entirely caused by us — humans. In fact, 99 percent of currently threatened species are at risk from human activities, primarily those driving habitat loss, introduction of exotic species, and global warming. Because the rate of change in our biosphere is increasing, and because every species' extinction potentially leads to the extinction of others bound to that species in a complex ecological web, numbers of extinctions are likely to snowball in the coming decades as ecosystems unravel.

AMPHIBIANS; Scientists estimate that a third or more of all the roughly 6,300 known species of amphibians are at risk of extinction. The current amphibian extinction rate may range from 25,039 to 45,474 times the background extinction rate.

BIRDS; Globally, Bird Life International estimates that 12 % of known 9,865 bird species are now considered threatened, with 192 species, or 2 percent, facing an "extremely high risk" of extinction in the wild — two more species than in 2008.

FISH; Across the globe, 1,851 species of fish — 21% of all fish species evaluated — were deemed at risk of extinction by the IUCN in 2010, including more than a third of sharks and rays.

INVERTEBRATES; Of the 1.3 million known invertebrate species, the IUCN has evaluated about 9,526 species, with about 30% of the species evaluated at risk of extinction.

MAMMALS; Overall, the IUCN estimates that half the globe's 5,491 known mammals are declining in population and a fifth are clearly at risk of disappearing forever with no less than 1,131 mammals across the globe classified as endangered, threatened, or vulnerable.

PLANTS; Of the more than 300,000 known species of plants, the IUCN has evaluated only 12,914 species, finding that about 68% of evaluated plant species are threatened with extinction.
Already, scientists say, warming temperatures are causing quick and dramatic changes in the range and distribution of plants around the world. With plants making up the backbone of ecosystems and the base of the food chain, that's very bad news for all species, which depend on plants for food, shelter, and survival.

REPTILES; Globally, 21% of the total evaluated reptiles in the world are deemed endangered or vulnerable to extinction by the IUCN — 594 species

Source: http://www.biologicaldiversity.org/programs/biodiversity/ elements_of_biodiversity/extinction_crisis/

THINK
THINK
THINK

BENDERSKUM THOUGHTS

Benderskum thoughts

Will you feel bloated on Christmas day? I hope not much food will get thrown away

I know it will though it's always like that and the one percents wallets still get fat

While down at the bottom and out on the street there are very many people that can't afford to eat

Now this is a fact a cast iron truth it's really fucking hard when you live by nail and tooth

I know cos i have been there and seen it through these eyes there's more to life than 9 to 5 that's slavery in disguise

My life outside the boundaries made me look way far beyond and I know it is quite hard to think like that in this totally clogged up pond

My life outside the boundaries was hard but it was free and if I'd never lived it I doubt that I'd be me

In the winter all my clothing would be frosted to the floor

But soon enough with a spliff in my gob I'd make the burner roar

In just my boots I'd hang my clothes above it in the heat

Lucky for me I lived deep in the woods and not on a city street

So off for a piss I'd wander a little way from home

Stark bullock fucking naked frozen to the bone

If you live on the streets it's just as cold and probably colder still

Cos you wouldn't have a homemade wood burner to take away the chill

So living on the streets was not a choice for me

Because I'm a born survivor and know what it is to be free

Not something I intended not something I had planned

But this could happen to anyone I hope you understand

I used to work with gardens and trees and I really loved my job

And quite a few bits of dangerous work but I earned a fair few bob
One night my vehicle was stolen and all my tools were taken
That fucked my work from there on in couldn't bring home the bacon
Well being a veggie that wasn't too bad
and as for the rest well, it could've been sad
I lived in a nice flat full of my stuff and sold it all for a ton
then watched him struggle to carry it out and smiled when it was done
I travelled round the country I even went to France
Well I actually woke up on a train by some strange circumstance
I went into town to a hippy bar someone put something in my drink
At least that's how I ended up there in France is all I can think
I got nicked in Ostend for what they thought was being rude
To a pair of proper ugly blokes a pair of uniformed dudes
I wasn't that rude just having some fun
Then they got quite pissed off and pointed their guns
That just made me laugh more.
Oh! It has to be said at this point in my life I was proper off my head
I sang Hari Krishna with my hands on my head
That angered them more their faces went bright red
The more I laughed the worse it got
The uniformed dudes were losing the plot
A crowd starts to form and a cop car arrives
Out from the car jumps an officer guy
I had machine pistols prodding my ribcage but decided the gorillas were bluffing
On reflection I guess it was lucky for me the new guy's hobby was cuffing
Much to the displeasure of the red faced buffoons
Their officer arrived to relieve them too soon
So there was I in a car with some cops
Its gets far, far worse it just never stops
They said there had been a burglary and they thought it might be

me
But I didn't fit the description so soon they let me free
Maybe you only just guessed maybe you knew all along
My life was little bit sketchy back then like a dodgy 80s song
So somehow I came to my senses or maybe I deeper dug
I loved my herb as I always have but danced to another drug
Went to many raves with a pill seller my lost best friend Yella
With me nearby looking mean as fuck it looked like I was the fella
Can you imagine me looking mean as fuck?
Not these days baby you're out of luck
In a car I travelled in style for a while with a girl and we lived in my tent
She simply did my head in with tarot and I ended up living in Kent
Doing my head in, how could that be?
A reading, for how do you want your tea?
So I moved to a place called Penny Pot Wood
I lived very simply as I knew that I could
That's when I found the place where I belong
That my dears is another fucking song

BOLLOTICS

Do recognise this? And I'm not just taking the piss
Honestly, I'm not joking it isn't fun that I'm poking
Just my comment on a system that's clearly broken
The masses carefully listen, but then, after the man has spoken
There's no solace to be found
None of that sacred middle ground
Not even a hint of any compromise
Just another pile of political lies
Or if you want be to be blunt
Because I'm a proper mouthy…bloke
Did I say it wasn't fun I poke?
Well what if I said that what I said was merely a mirror image?
And then suggest because it rhymes we play a game of scrimmage
No forget that rhyming for the sake it annoys the fuck out of poets
I've seen
So I'm doing it here just to be mean
Anyway before I digress further still and lose my track completely
Oh shit too late there was a point but what it was defeats me
It's ok though nonsense has no true direction
It's all perhaps merely a complete deflection
Word masturbation for the want of a better
Mounting excitement with every single letter
One finger typing it's taking too long
There was the point Oh shit it's gone
Pointless drivel saying nothing of any import
The trap is set, words the bait, you were caught
Why oh why can I not fly?
Said the broken ninja butterfly
You can fly said a strangely normal sort of guy

Silhouetted by the moon in the midnight sky
Do you remember him in the hobnail suit?
Watching the bear eating peach tree root
No worries all good probably nonsense like of which I spoke
Now back to that feeling that it shouldn't be fun that I poke
Or poke that I fun one or the other or the other or one
I'm not sure anymore I think it's my head that I've spun

NO MORE PLANT BASED

Suddenly plant based vegans abound
To make corporations a pretty pound
So the people at the top
Decided to alter the shop
Plant based foods galore
However a few things more
Extra added ingredients
Not for your convenience
Quorn is vile I have to say
80% of its RNA
Needs removing to make it edible
A fact I find totally incredible
Faky baky plant based meat
Food for the fledgling vegans to eat
A different poison an a different plate
While the shops make profit at a higher rate
Plant based burgers that seem to bleed
A new agenda for corporate greed
Don't eat that plant based meat it's fucking disgusting
If you believe it's healthy you're obviously very trusting
The Westminster psychopaths once again have turned their back
on the needy
While stuffing their faces in parliament because they are much,
much more than greedy
They give themselves a pay rise because it's what they need
It takes a special person with a special sort of greed
Monty Python summed them up with the character Mr. Creosote
They stuff their faces all day long until their bellies bloat
They don't give a toss when children in fact they probably gloat
But there is a way to put this right

An end to the government's greedy shite
The government do not care us and think they are being shrewd
Thinking that they have fooled us all they are extremely fucking rude
Resource based economy is the way of the future
An old new way that's much more effective than a suture
Don't be fooled grow your food
In the ground life renewed
Plant a seed, watch it grow and before long you'll have food
Without adding to the bank balance of the extremely fucking rude

NUMBERS

Don't worry about a number; especially the number six
It's used a lot in geomantics a special box of tricks
It's not about a deck of cards or a set of wooden sticks
It's just about a number a special box of tricks
In signs it can be good or bad depending on your outlook
The sort of thing that lives within and not from a dusty textbook
If you doubt what I say read it yourself from a textbook if you must
Just remember though cast iron opinions can also turn to rust
When you use a basic layout of sixes in this divinatory tale
Don't try to tell me its bollocks because trust me on this you will fail
So the fact that I just made it up doesn't mean it isn't true
Is it just nonsense or bollocks I leave that entirely to you

Fortuna Minor~success~ at least a small goal, possibly intentional as it removes the view from the bigger picture
Let them eat cake and remember this hollow empty gesture over well everything really. But success is still just that
Amissio~loss~a bad sign in all things material as in societie's gates but for love it is good due to its intangible nature, so for the material world stuff is just stuff it comes and it goes time to put some back and start growing once more
Carcer~prison~denotes set backs or failure maybe of society as a whole and is a path to a new beginning. Even within confines there is the spirit of hope not everyone will give up and despair as society crumbles and the walls break down between us, psycho-

44

logical walls that are there to divide and conquer us, but all things turn to dust

Conjunctio~crossroads~but neutral six denoting continuation good in good bad in bad, so if it's this six wherever you go there you are. Continue to strive for good and good will prevail or continue to wallow in failure and let that be your path

Acqusitio~grain~this is good for it represents seeds for the future and growth and as the fifth of the six in question represents this where it leads to Resource Based Economy RBE, shopsNOTcrops, free food for all and the end to the capitalist dream, which of course can only lead to;

Fortuna Major~greater fortune~blessings from the earth even after the world has been robbed of much splendour rebirth and renewal will follow and nature will prevail, so what you need to do is just be on the winning side

Treasure our World it's the only one we have

So no need to worry 6 is a good number probably

Cannamaste

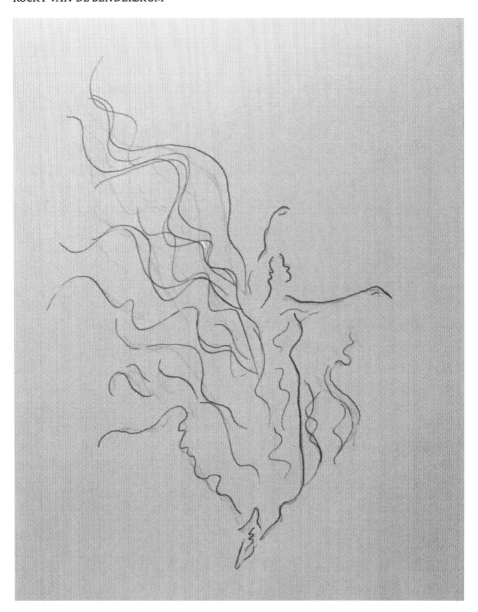

NOT VEGAN BECAUSE

Hypnotised vegan meets a half cloned boy and it plays on her mind quite a lot
The half cloned boy sat around with a grin and smoked huge amounts of pot
She's actually not a vegan because secretly she eats
Packets and packets and packets of those squishy jelly sweets
Even though they are disgusting and made of lips and bums and feet
Which she surely can't really believe while eating those sugary treats
In a show of phony empathy she eats her vegan meat
If you listen she'll always blame others she's nothing but a cheat
Although not just her, he's just as bad trendy fucking vegan lad
He's got muscles and He's vegan He's proper fucking rad
He proudly eats his plant based meat and thinks that he cool
The corporations reel him in another blinded fool
Plant based meat is disgusting although that's merely my opinion
Other people can do what they like their bodies aren't my domin-
ion
In maccy dees or kayefsees or even murder things
Calling it delicious like vegan puppets on invisible corporate strings
I do however like veggie bangers and veggie burgers too
But to make it appear to be bleeding makes me wanna spew
When you tell me that you like, your veggie burger bleeding
If you're trying to disgust me then trust you are succeeding
Just to clarify this point in case you gave it a miss
Fast food companies are not ethical and really take the piss
So labelling it vegan friendly isn't friendly to animals still
The only ones it's friendly to reap profits from the till

It's all a massive shop where they think everything's for sale
But there are those us of still price tag less and we're here to watch
them fail
Grow your own food and grow so much you have to give it away
The end of this capitalist society is near and that'll be the day

NONSENSICAL

It may all seem like nonsense but believe me there's no duplicity
I get this shocking feeling and I don't mean like electricity
I'm a simple fucking benderskum and there's nothing that I hate
However don't put strawberries or fake meat on my plate
I also exclude almonds and any yoghurt too
I will either be allergic or projectile fucking spew
Now buttons you know are dangerous and sap you of your health
Crop circles are the same but are always made by stealth
But drumming fucking circles that's another weird dimension
They make me feel like spazzing and I don't mean dynamic tension
Beaches are another where so much rubbish has been thrown
Don't think I'll grow to like all that stuff that bird has long since flown
I guess most of you like showers not me not one little bit
The only thing that angers me and make me want to hit
Is having stuff sprayed at my face for me it is zero fun
Give if it a try if you really must but then I suggest you run
You wouldn't like me when I'm angry although I don't turn green
From calm as fuck to apocalyptically violent without an in between
So six a song of sixpence a pocket full of rye
Splash my face with anything I'll poke you in the eye
Humpty dumpty sat on a wall eating a blackbird pie
Along came a spider that sat down beside her and poked her in the eye
Oh but maybe you were not aware that humpty is a girl
Old King Cole was a merry old soul, as he watched the rhymes unfurl
Mary, Mary quite contrary how does your garden grow?

Well, Jack and Jill went up the hill so I don't fucking know
What was that shit all about? A total load of drivel
Rock a bye baby on the treetop can you feel your brain start to
shrivel
I often try to warn you all about the power of words
However all think I'm joking or think that it's absurd
I only try to warn because I know you don't like danger
But whatever doesn't kill you will certainly make you stranger

LAND OF HOPELESS TORY

Land of Hopeless Tory, just don't pretend you're free,
how shall we extort thee, to make us more money?

Wider still, and wider, shall our wallets get;
you might think we're nasty but you ain't seen nothing yet!

Truth and Right and Freedom, ever heard of them?
Talks of political rightness, makes me hawk up phlegm.

Tho' thy way be darkened, and you feel depressed,
we will sell your services and feather our own nest.

Stacked up with the billions, we make for our mates,
We keep you all divided and smile at racial hate.

Land of Hopeless Tory, just don't pretend you're free,
how shall we extort thee, to make us more money?

Hark, once mighty nation don't bother to reply;
Low, is how we view you, low, whilst we are high!

Even if you support us, you will feel the sting;
As we sell your freedom, along with everything!

HOW DID WE ALL
GET HERE, HOW HAS
THIS BECOME?

Why is the environment so far down it should be number one?
In the list I mean of important things
But it's not over till the fat lady sings
The fat lady being Gaia or maybe mother earth
The maker of life the place of our birth
Many are missing empathy or at least that's how it seems
Ignoring the pain and suffering deafened to the screams
They have no care for other species or the sanctity of life
When their food is killed in a slaughterhouse or cut with a very
sharp knife
But it isn't only animals we are killing for bit by bit
We are suffocating our biosphere with evermore plastic shit
We're filling up the oceans and poisoning the land
There is no planet B in sight what don't they understand?
An ancient prophesy I once read said money can't be eaten
But try to get that understood by those who were schooled at
Eton
Or any manufacturer of the modern political elite
That prepares them to fall asleep in another leather seat

HARVEST FESTIVAL
CROPS NOT SHOPS

Resource based economy we won't be stopped
We're a growing movement yet not new on the scene
Intending the ending of the capitalists dream
They have tried to control the people's food
But they can fuck off or is that too rude
I don't really care I'm not here to impress you
But join in our movement you know I will bless you
We grow what we like and we like what we grow
But there's one vital point I think you should know
We don't run for money that's a thing of the past
Autonomy is coming autocracy won't last
They won't like our actions and just try thwart us
With right on our side and nature to support us
We know that we can only prevail
Capitalism is doomed and will soon start to fail

GOBBLEDEGOOK;

*A book advertising a poem; or
a poem advertising a book*

This is to anyone that likes my poetry;
I just make it up so to speak in all honesty
Whatever you think you saw or you read
Believe when I say it came straight from my head
So for what you just heard I refuse to take blame
You may not have heard right so it gives me no shame
I wish I was someone who is known to be clever
Like that bloke in the song you know him name of Trevor
But the fact is clever is something I ain't
And I only write this stuff on the days I can't paint
I don't really plan the stuff that I write
Therefore it may come out sounding like shite
I never get worried over what's in my head
I jot it all down so it may well get read
However I is proper prolific when my broken body let's me
At least it is with scribbling and I do that quite intensely
My mind would allow it all of the time
But when my body hurts I do it in rhyme
Its gobbledegook and nonsense see
And I'm very glad it's out of me
PHEW!

If you get my drift or not it's okay
If I'm a bit short of oil and I don't mean olay
My mind can write gibberish all day long

And if you're not careful I may sing a song
Satirical politics that's sometimes how I roll
It may not be that funny but I still find it droll
If you take me too seriously I suggest you just scroll
Down to find secret smiles that you obviously hide
There they are to make some more Anandemide
So you see then my poetry just isn't real
Just some rambling on about the way that I feel
Sometimes it's nonsense cos I feel that way too
Or gobbledegook but I still think that's true
But if you do like it that is also quite fine
Just as long as you realise not all poetry rhymes
And not all rhyming words should be considered poetic
In fact sometimes something way more prophetic
Was all of that lying or was some of it true?
That foot's firmly entrenched in a totally different shoe

THE WORLD NEEDS
A HAND

I love it that more and more people are turning to gardening and growing their own food but please bear this in mind;

I can see a huge ecological nightmare in the making caused by all the non recyclable plastic plant pots around, that all the garden centres and the like use.

There's an alternative to this that I'll come back to in a bit.

There are these days ways of remaking that non-recyclable plastic, unfortunately our governments don't give a shit as long as their pockets are full.

In the Netherlands they have been repairing roads with recycled plastic pellets, but that's again a short term problem as that stuff breaks down to micro plastic which once it gets into the sea is literally getting stuck in the throats of plankton and killing it off.

I'll link a video of this happening to this blah, blah, blah

It used to be a fact that some plastics could not be recycled and reused elsewhere so did they stop making those ones and only make reusable ones? No, of course they didn't that stuff was cheap and it made them dosh, also many of the people that were put in place to protect and preserve our world had no real interest in what they are doing.

On the ground roots level many do it's just they are often thwarted by lesser humans higher up in the administrative pecking order.

Though not always but I'll come to that in a minute.

Nowadays processes have been invented to reuse all that shit. It's here so it needs to be in use otherwise it breaks down and well you'll see if watch the attached video

However a far better and much more sustainable option would be to stop making the stuff and by that stuff I mean, plastics made from fossil fuels that are only degradable which means it can only become many smaller parts and yes I realise fossil fuels isn't scientifically correct as someone once pointed out while I was blah, blah, blahing,

As opposed to biodegradable where it becomes soil from where it came. I don't mean we can turn soil into plastic and with the shortage of actual soil on the planet it would be disastrous if somebody invented such a process. I think you would be amazed at how little soil we have on the planet to grow our food in and before anyone suggests hydroponics and aquaponics these processes lack molybdenum which is essential for our full uptake of nutrients from our food. We get it from eating plants grown in soil and of course some get it from eating animals that have eaten plants grown in the soil. The only way it could ever be in a hydraponic or aquaponic growing system is by adding it but to add it we need the soil to extract it from in the first place. Post second world war farming practices depleted the soil available at vast rates till we now have I hear 80 years of soil left at current rates of depletion. So it's time to put back what we have taken. It's like scraping the skin of a potato soon it will only be potato left without skin our world is the potato where we live is the skin.

What we don't need to do is ask our government for the help they would only give at quite a cost. What we do need to do is help ourselves and each other, to become more sustainable, by both practical help and passed on knowledge.

I for instance have a lifetime of experience half of which you wouldn't believe and I love imparting knowledge but my practical skills are next to zero these days, but whatever

Back to the attitude of the mechanisms in place;

A few years ago I got a bee in my bonnet about TetraPaks and how wasteful it was they just went to landfill.

So I contacted the manufacturers of the packs, I was very surprised at their response.

They were very nice and very eco conscious they told me the packs are made of 16 parts each one can be recycled and used again and they have a machine which does exactly that. I was impressed but still not satisfied. So I asked why nobody recycles them in Britain if there are machines to do it are they too expensive not ecologically but economically.

The next bit I was shocked by they said they have offered a machine to councils across the country but only very few had taken them up on their offer. The machine was offered free of charge and maintained for five years free of charge, wow I thanked him and said I'd be back in touch.

I then started phoning councils time consuming as you can imagine if you've ever had to suffer a council telephone queuing system blaring Vivaldi or 80s pop songs in your ear, you'll know how patient I am. When I say councils I mean everywhere England, Scotland, Wales and Northern Ireland, eventually I knew which route was the quickest, I guess whoever installed the first lot of them got the contract. Now do I mean telephone systems or the operatives, who knows?

The answer I got from most was it was only free for five years, which was frustrating to say the least. So I decided on a different route and got to the environmental officers as being in the same field they would have often studied at the same universities so would be part of a larger network.

They got on it I was way happy that I'd passed it on to someone that would use and was in the job because they cared. I'd done my little bit and was happy about it. Some of the councils back then still gave the job to a member of staff completely unqualified, as the environment became more and more of a thing with the establishment.

You may think that an odd thing to say but I used to work as a subcontractor for the Department of the Environment and whenever I suggested doing something different to their accepted standard and quite environmentally damaging they all just thought I was a nutter. To be fair that's not too foreign an observation but they thought it because I cared about my world they just had a job, it was really a massive estate agent the department I mean they just managed all the government's properties and places belonging to the people as gifts from previous owners like Stonehenge. Anyway that's just to get you to the notion that they don't care about the environment, because I don't believe they do and I'm sure as shit not the only one.

So back to the start I'm so glad more and more people are realising actually how easy it is to grow your own food and also how tasty that food is. Plus the more you grow the better you get at it and with communities all growing food to share everyone gains from the shared knowledge initially then eventually that becomes general knowledge.

Just before I finish I want to mention Hemp Plastic, obviously hemp, cannabis, marijuana, weed or any of the other names I like them all if you know me, you'll know that.

All plant plastic but hemp because of its myriad of other uses besides plastic. I don't even mean whole monocrop hemp fields I mean diversity hemp repairs but we still need the rest, so hemp fields amongst the other fields, proper just like it was and just like it should be. Why isn't well you can only grow it with a licence and although obtainable not that easily however what nonsense is that you have to have a licence to grow a crop. Is the infrastructure of our country so heavily invested in unsustainable practices that a plant with so many possibilities could threaten their status quo.

Anyway I digress again just this;

Anything made from Hydrocarbons

Can also be made from Carbohydrates

But things made from Carbohydrates biodegrade but due to processes that clever people understand not benderskum all we know is the oil we call fossil oil really come from dead organisms like algae and zooplankton that existed millions of years ago in the sea. But I'm just a benderskum and might have just made it all up.

We want to encourage people to live in a way that is not only sustainable to themselves but also to their world and vice versa. The better you live the better you live, the worse you live the worse you live and wherever you go there you are.

I realise not everybody has the opportunity to grow their food at home but we are encouraging community food allotments and gardens.
Free food for all and a resourced based economy for a more sustainable future.

EVEN MORE DRIVEL

Look out ears here it comes
Rocky van de fucking Benderskum
Its gob never stops spouting shite
Not even in the middle of the night
But what is it talking about? Nobody knows
You'd get more sense from a murder of crows
Yes, you've guessed it just like every other time
Lines of drivel that sometimes even rhyme
Does it care if you like its style?
Not these days, nor for quite a fucking while
Did I swear? Well I am a fouled mouthed twat
That's not gonna change so think about that
Some people listen although they can't hear
Communication is not always clear
Some people hear but never listen because that bit is done with
the brain
The senses combined can lead you astray and make you appear
quite insane
So balance is needed or homeostasis or even the goldilocks zone
I personally get this from marijuana and I know that I'm not alone
My personal use isn't for pain relief it's really cos I love being
stoned
Not throwing rocks but high on bud, the other sort I think I'd have
moaned
For me pain relief is a secondary thing but better than potions and
pills
That will only exacerbate the problem without ever curing your
ills
Anyway back to the point of this blah-blah-blah
Was to talk about nothing and I've managed it so far

But now for the usual obviously needed and legal serious part
Every word you've read so far costs a fiver and that's right from
the start
If you're lucky and only saw this video of drivel
You're probably safe and your bank balance won't shrivel
Except I have a friend a Romanian hacker named Goran
He swears blind he's Scottish and wears a kilt and a sporran
Plus the language he speaks is something quite well…foreign

Now where was I again oh yeah Forgetfulness 101
Keep them there waiting for a point just for the sake of fun
Then babble on endlessly for hours and hours without ever com-
ing to that point
Then sometimes at least if you know what I mean take a break for
a well earned joint
These days there's so much to talk about most of it boring as fuck
We won't wipe ourselves out just yet it seems at least with a bit of
luck
So if you've managed to get this far I hope you enjoyed the ride
If though, you are reading this 'PAY THE FUCK UP' and don't even
bother to hide
We hacked your phone when you started watching with our new
technology
So even our video viewers are fucked our sincerest apologies
Cannamaste

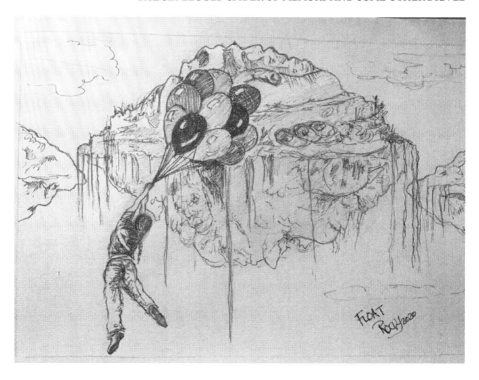

BE SEVENTEENTH
HEMP TESTER

An epic journey for a benderskum as walking is painful as fuck
But building back muscle quite slowly with a little bit of luck
Coffee and Avo Sarny, this benderskum is out to lunch
'Tea & Times' is the name of the place a really friendly bunch
I've not done this for ages it seems like a different life
These days if you believe the media it's nothing but trouble and strife
What's more the cash in my pocket was as welcome as any old card
What did shops do last year; think about it, if that action isn't too hard
It is what it is because we allowed it, so there's nobody else to blame
Those that conceived all the misinformations are no doubt devoid of all shame
We know the government don't lie they are straight as straight as a dye
If you honestly believe my last sentence say it back as you look in my eye
I can recognise your false agenda and see you're not telling the truth
I've been on this rock a minute or two and I'm way too long in the tooth
So that was my journey and painful it was
I stopped now and then but only… because
I wanted to post a couple of books so decided to do it by shanks
This is the stuff I do to myself I'm the butt of most of my pranks
I wake up most mornings struggling to breathe

If you hadn't experienced you wouldn't believe
It's like a hammer is hitting me in the chest
Or several shots in my bulletproof vest
Which I don't really have I hasten to add
I interject. Oops, sorry, my bad!
It's hard to explain but it feels a bit like drowning
If there was someone with me and on my back they were pounding
In my head I know for a fact if you did that it would make it go away
So if you read this and see me choking remember the fact I asked you to store away
I didn't do any shopping there is nothing I need so I didn't have queue anywhere
Except in the post office but lucky for there was also a convenient chair
Then back to the sofa to sit and translate this drivel disguised as poetry
Don't try to tell me it grows on you drivel is drivel can't you see?
Nevertheless I'll continue to write it
The urge is inside me I'm not gonna fight it
Better out than in I was told and conveniently believe
Better than any other throw away saying hiding up my sleeve
Speaking of sleeves my jacket ripped, its coming apart at the seams
Time to get another I guess while I've still got the ways and the means

FOOD FOR THE FUTURE

Food for the future these days is what it's all about
No need for to protest get out there holler and shout
So these days front line protesting are not the thing for me
I'd rather earth my potatoes up and plant a lemon tree
And sit amongst the strawberries I'll grow, even though I think they're vile
Vegetables and fruit grown in the soil not missing that vital ingredient
The absence of which in hydroponic farms is maybe truly expedient
Without this element in our diet we can't take all the vital nutrition
So effectively making us weaker with no need for a war of attrition
It goes quite deep it's well thought out this wanton war on food
If you thought the GMO was bad well that was way too crude
That's not for us we have good soil
With a lot of care and bit of toil
We intend to grow exponentially
Whilst treating our world reverentially
No chemicals needed to poison the ground
Organic practices that are vegan and sound
Trees full of fruit and hedges too
Food for free the whole year through

EAT THE GOVERNMENT

So what of this corona of which they all speak
Has it had its day has it reached its peak?
Did they mention a vaccine mandatory injection?
Or is that just another form of baffling misdirection
Will they give us all trackers as part of this jab?
Cos a needle that big would leave quite a scab
I'll give you this next for you to be mulling
I believe they think our numbers need culling
Maybe I'm just spouting another conspiracy
All very possible after all I'm out of warrantee
Or perhaps I'm looking at the lesson of recent history
It don't really matter we likes a little mystery
Social distance unless you are hunting
At weddings it seems less guests and more bunting
What's occurring in government is way more sinister
With a lying, racist, homophobic prime minister
Brother and bob here's your head on a plate
Stuffing the purses of family and mates
Oh! Is this one of ours? Who bids a pound?
If you think that I'm joking just stick around
I can't really see their logic and their aim is not very clear
Except to control us like slaves using an inbuilt fear
Fear of the unknown is a human trait and a very powerful tool
When you speak out loud of this unknown fear you may sound like a fool
So instead you keep quiet and follow along
Whether for them or rebel it's still the same old song
I hear murmurs here and there and talk of revolution
That just shuffles things around so is not a real solution
Change the very narrative right down to the core

Don't play them at their own game, turn away, ignore
In a capitalists society everything is a shop
So give it away don't sell it and make that nonsense stop
When was it decided I'd work eight hours every day
To make somebody a fortune for very little pay
Work like a slave while you think you are free
I stepped away from it, that's just not for me
Career politicians are what I believe is the trouble
They have no life experience democracy born in a bubble
These days though firsthand knowledge doesn't count for very much
As long as you accept a back handshake and practice Double Dutch
I seemed to have wandered off topic in fact I can't ever remember
The topic I mean that fire went out aeons ago and there's not even a glowing ember
I won't bother to try to regain my thread but leave you to do the math
Just tell you this little story about a Westmonster psychopath
This government's history is a treasure trove
Listen to the words of Michael Gove
Animals he said feel no pain
Now that's a statement quite insane
I wrote a little poem about that very thing
It was found on my laptop by my very good friend String
It's called "Goodnights to Human Rights"
Not really suitable for the garden of delights
Animals it seems feel no pain unless they live in France or Spain
Or anywhere else that isn't insane but in Britain the animals feel no pain
If you think that's a joke there's worse to come your rights eroded by political scum
Ignore what is said behind their election pitches
They'll do what they like without any hitches
The salesman tells you when it's gone it's gone
And...there go your rights one by one

Hark at the sounds of insidious laughter
A feudal system is what they're really after
They really don't listen to me or you
They were voted in and they'll do what they do
Back to the animals who they say feel no pain
They consider us animals we're one and the same

Eat the Government

CROPS NOT SHOPS

I want to introduce these folks they really are the tops
A proper growing community they call it Crops Not Shops
They've been around in Essex helping people grow
For food is a right for all of us something you should know
In gardens, allotments and a nursery and now down on an animal farm
Though not where they breed the animals for food these are safe from harm
The place near Ashford in deepest Kent is a place that's hard to beat
A wonderful Animal Sanctuary beginning with Retreat
I went along to give advice? That's all I have the strength to give
I loved the way the animals are and how they get to live
The poly tunnel frame put up by a valiant bunch of workers
While I sat down and watched because trust I'm a proper shirker
If my body wasn't so broken I know I could be handy
But this is the body that I've got so sitting down is dandy
So all I can do is sit and watch and try to give advice
I'd be helping if I had different one you needn't ask me twice
So all I can do is write this stuff and watch the world go by
As the poly tunnel is constructed under the bright blue sky
The farm itself is brilliant the staff were all amazing
It's lush to see happy animals wandering around and grazing
They have a thrift shop and a café with vegan friendly food
I never mentioned my cannibal diet as it seemed a little rude
I know that I will go back down to help whenever I can
I'll probably grab a plate or two of that lovely vegan scran
The farm is very popular as its one of those special places
When some of the visitors find its vegan food the looks upon their faces

One thing I really liked to hear was none of the food is ever wasted
Because they have pigs to eat the scraps but never themselves to be tasted
Now back to the tribe and the growing of crops when the poly tunnel is built
Organic vegetables and maybe fruit filled up to the hilt
And a biogas digester but I'm not really sure what that is
I was told but it went right over my head its ok I can give it a miss
For I'm a simple benderskum and there are some things I know
One of them is Crops not Shops is a thing that is bound to grow

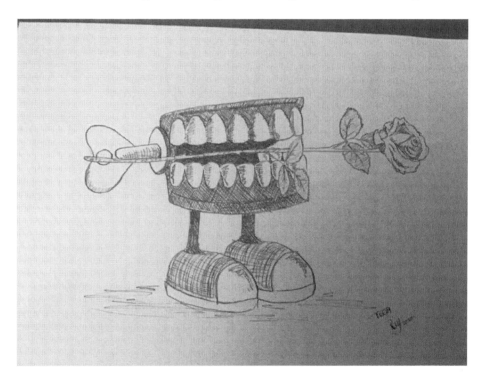

BOLLOCKS TO DRUMS

I'll give you a little insight into this little benderskum
Cos you seem to think I'm marching to the beat of a different drum
When you say I march to the beat of a different fucking drum
I reply I never march so stick that up your bum
If you knew me well enough you'd know I'd always say
Bollocks to your drums every single day
Although I really do love Drum n fuckin Bass
Djembes in my world have no fucking place
 Drum circles made me want to fully projectile vomit
If there is a planet B I wish they'd go and drum on it
Didgereedon'ts the same and penny whistles too
Forky Nippy music that makes me wanna spew
They say my beat is different not Pa rum pum pum pum
Trust me I don't march at all and there is no fucking drum
So now it seems the monkey is crawling from the sleeve
Every time you start to drum I simply want to leave
There was a lone and loony guy that started to play a drum
He couldn't play I have to say and I hope some more don't come
When they start those drumming circles it makes me want to heave
So I doff my hat and pull on my coat and quickly fucking leave
I get no pleasure hearing Pa rum pum pum pum
So grasp your djembe firmly and stuff it up your bum

#ARTYNOT

Apparently that's all very well if you're arty but that's something I definitely ain't

I know that some people would disagree after seeing the stuff that I paint

However that is all just practice and one day I'll get it done right

Until then I'll scribble in paint and words and leave you to think it's not shite

If you have even a hairs breadth of artisticliness you'll know I'm telling the truth

I've scribbled in 7 different decades and I'm somewhat long in the tooth

Many think I'm a foul mouthed twat that should wash out its mouth with soap

Some folks though listen to the words behind words the others just don't have a hope

If you know me you'll know I'm an anarchist and think anarchy is what our world needs

The way it is being plundered it's a wound that continues to bleed

I don't believe in riches or I own more stuff than you

That shits proper outdated and has been for a century or two

Yet still the government try to treat us all like serfs

But going to a public school doesn't give you extra worth

And say blah, blah, blah for the rest

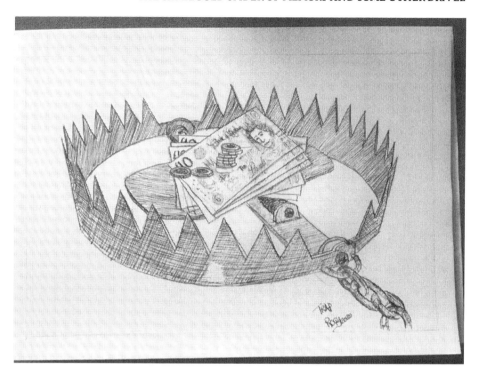

JUST BECAUSE I CAN

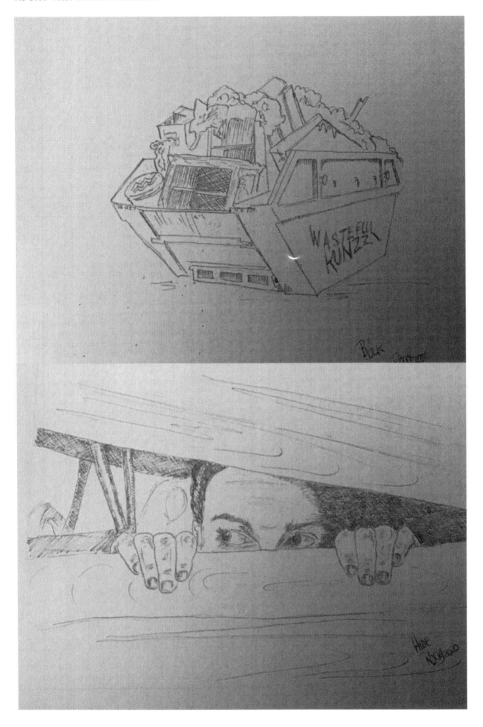

AFTERWORD

This book has been lovingly created with all expenses spared apart from the cost of some tofu

ABOUT THE AUTHOR

Rocky Van De Benderskum

A benderskum
That doesn't drum

BOOKS BY THIS AUTHOR

What's In A Benderskum

A book of drivel

String's Book Of A Benderskum

Yet more drivel

Printed in Poland
by Amazon Fulfillment
Poland Sp. z o.o., Wrocław